For Fans of

LEVEN THUMPS

PROFESSOR WINSNICKER'S

❈

BOOK OF PROPER ETIQUETTE FOR WELL-MANNERED

❈

SYCOPHANTS

As kept by
CLOVER ERNEST

Recovered by
OBERT SKYE

Marvelously Written and Clearly Instructional

Visit us at shadowmountain.com and LevenThumps.com

Library of Congress Cataloging-in-Publication Data
Skye, Obert.
    Professor Winsnicker's book of proper etiquette for well-mannered
sycophants / Obert Skye.
        p. cm.
    Summary: A textbook explaining the proper behavior of sycophants
in the land of Foo, along with journal entries kept by a young
sycophant named Clover Ernest, who will become the sycophant of
Leven Thumps.
    ISBN-13: 978-1-59038-716-0 (hardbound : alk. paper)
    [1. Diaries—Fiction. 2. Fantasy.] I. Title.
    PZ7.S62877Pr 2007
    [Fic]—dc22   2006033466

Printed in the United States of America
Worzalla Publishing Co., Stevens Point, WI

10   9   8   7   6   5   4   3   2   1

Publisher's Preface

When Obert Skye first brought us the story of Leven Thumps, we were certain it was a product of his imagination and insisted on publishing it as fiction. But now he has given us additional evidence of Foo in the form of a textbook/journal belonging to the sycophant Clover Ernest.

In order to present this material to the world in its purest, most convincing form, we opted not to re-typeset but simply to reproduce the pages as they appeared in the book found by Obert. Clover's doodles and Obert's personal handwritten notes have thus been preserved. The pages also include a "lost chapter" that was not printed in the original text, which Clover evidently discovered on one of his forays into Professor Winsnicker's office drawers.

The particular treasures of this text, though, are the journal entries kept by Clover, which have been preserved in his own handwriting. This firsthand look at Foo through the eyes of one of its inhabitants will hopefully convince skeptics once and for all of the existence of this magical place.

HOW THIS BOOK CAME TO BE

I have met very few people I didn't like. There was that one fellow with the long, sharp knife, and that tall woman with the beyond-bad attitude, and of course all those who fight against Foo, but for the most part I find people agreeable.

That is not the case with Terry Graphs. He is despicable, mean, cruel, and—on the occasions when I have had the misfortune of being near him—smelly. So it was with some concern and yet great excitement that I contacted him after seeing what he had posted for sale on eBay. His ad read:

Old dumb book—wife thinks it's worth something. Written by Foo, or a professor, or a sycophant, whoever that is. Found on the

Oklahoma prairie not far from where our
house was demolished. I personally discovered it while picking up the pieces of the
single-wide I still owe on. You tell me what
you'll pay for it and we might have a deal.

I flew to Oklahoma and happily bought the
book from him for thirty dollars and the silver watch
I was wearing. Terry had no idea what he had found
or what he was selling. He also had very pungent
breath.

I have studied the book for many months now.
The best I can figure is that sometime during
Clover's stay in Reality it fell from his void, or perhaps he was looking at it on the prairie and foolishly
left it behind. Either way, we are lucky. There are
many things about Foo and the sycophants that can
be gleaned from it.

Read it carefully. It is a tremendous glimpse into
the mind and life of Leven's faithful friend Clover.

Fate was kind to drop it in my lap. Of course,
luckily for all of us, fate seems to favor Foo.

Obert Skye

Table of Great Contents

(Though it may be tempting to read ahead, sticking with the prescribed and masterfully planned order will make you that much smarter.)

INTERESTING THAT THIS IS THE FIFTH CHAPTER

For the sake of convenience, and in an effort to immortalize my words, I have gone to the trouble of carving seven reminders into the trunk of the dead fantrum tree that stands outside my dwelling. I suggest you walk by and look at them often.

THE SEVEN SYCOPHANT REMINDERS

1. A sycophant is better neither seen nor heard—unless spoken to or questioned, in which case it is best that you speak up and answer politely.

2. A sycophant never bites and tells; it is not unheard of, however, to bite and draw a descriptive picture.

3. Hands off whatever distracts you. Look away from what holds your gaze. There are forces at work that would love to entrance you.

4. Thou shalt not be so vain as to care what you are called—unless you are renamed Roy, in which case you have decent argument for change.

5. Your house may shift, and you will enter many doors in your lifetime, but your home will always be Sycophant Run.

6. The secrets you learn, or those that already reside in your head, belong to you. If questioned about them, make something up.

7. Most important, take care, and remember that without you, Foo will fall.

FOO-RENOWNED
PROFESSOR PHILIP WINSNICKER

INSIGHTFUL INTRODUCTION

BY NONE OTHER THAN PROFESSOR PHILIP WINSNICKER HIMSELF

Greetings, my young sycophant, greetings. How fortunate you are to be holding such a magnificent book. How your mind must be shivering in anticipation of the great wisdom of which you are about to partake. I know *I* can hardly wait, and I wrote the book.

There is something special about being a sycophant. You are among the very most important inhabitants of Foo. I'm sure it gives you great pride when someone as scholarly as I points this fact out.

For the record, you are quite welcome.

We will cover a great deal in this book. It will be my task to leave no gap in your understanding. I suspect that under my tutelage, and by the time you read the very last page, you will be well on your way to understanding what is expected of you and just how you can become the most reliable sycophant possible.

It is with great foresight that I have anticipated your desire to keep copious notes as you read these teachings. I'm sure the things I am saying will spark endless discussion within your own head. Ergo, I am providing you a little space at the end of each chapter for you to write out just how much I have influenced you. I'm certain as you read and reread this book throughout your existence that you will find it immeasurably helpful and that your own comments, while not certifiably educated, will be cute in their own right.

I must warn you, however: Keep this book close

to you. Do not let it fall into the <u>wrong hands</u>. There are things about yourself and Sycophant Run that others would capture and curse for.

There are many who would love to get hold of this very book. Many souls would use the information within its pages to trick and flatter you. (Flattery, I must add, is one of the most blinding and deceitful of tricks.)

So please, my wonderful friend, use your great brain wisely and protect this book. Watch for eyes behind you or shadows hovering over you. Read the words to yourself. If the dirt beneath you is hissing, close your book and find a safer place to read. I know it will be tempting to quote and speak aloud the beautifully written text you are about to experience, but please, for the sake of all that is possible in Foo, do not. The very existence of your world and dreams could be shattered by your carelessness. Do not let this book out of your sight.

You have been warned.

On a much happier note, enjoy!

Professor Philip Winsnicker

HOW FORTUNATE THAT TERRY GRAPHS DIDN'T REALIZE WHAT HE ACTUALLY HAD!

L.W.

CHAPTER ONE

GROOMING AND ROBE MAINTENANCE

PREPARE YOUR MIND.
HERE COMES THE WISDOM.

Chances are, you are hairy. I've met only two sycophants who weren't, and I have personally discussed
things with them about their condition. You, however, have hair—everywhere. This is a good thing.
Although the two hairless sycophants I have met
claim it's quite nice not having to pick thorns and bit
bugs from their pelts, you will never really know if
they are telling the truth, because your condition is
hairy.

You were born with hair and someday, if you

HE MUST BE TALKING ABOUT THE FIDGET TWINS

1

PROFESSOR WINSNICKER'S PATENTED GROOMING COMB.

*Designed especially
for life's toughest tangles.*

Made from the finest fantrum wood.
Hand crafted by the cloistered sycophants
of the Worm Worn Mountains.

**One stroke and
you'll be hooked.**

A GIFT TO SYCOPHANTS EVERYWHERE:

*Not responsible for cuts and bruises brought about as a result of use.
If injured consult Professor Winsnicker for a thorough
explanation as to how you must have misused it.*

taste death, you will die with hair. So, since this is a fact of sycophant life, let us discuss just how best to groom yourself. With my superior intellect I can anticipate the question you are forming: "Professor, what does our appearance matter, seeing how we spend the majority of our time invisible?"

Excellent question.

Any dedicated sycophant spends the bulk of his or her day invisible. But when you do show yourself, it is to your great advantage to look your best. Oftentimes the appearance of a sycophant is a tremendous surprise. It is so much easier to the eyes to be surprised by a nice-looking, well-combed sycophant. I know that when I was snatched into Foo at the age of twenty-four, it was a comfort, however slight, to be greeted by my well-manicured sycophant, Harold. And even though I screamed and cried for hours, I can still remember thinking, "At least this funny creature takes care of himself."

Combing yourself at least once every couple of days will make both your appearance and your life more enjoyable.

First impressions are the longest lasting.

It doesn't take much time to look tip-top, not much time at all. I've found that the best way to work over your hair is with a Professor Winsnicker's Patented Grooming Comb—just the right size for most sycophant hands. The texture is pleasing to the grip and the combing action becomes almost fun.

ASK CLOVER IF HE STILL HAS HIS.

Place the Professor Winsnicker's Patented Grooming Comb in your right hand and begin at the top of your left side. With short, easy strokes begin to comb downward with spirit and gusto. Start at the head, move to the arm, end at the leg. Once you have finished with the left side, move the comb to the left hand and repeat the process on the right side. I've included an excellent illustration to best demonstrate my instruction.

You may encounter stubborn snags. Fear not, I am here to talk you through. When a snag occurs,

NOT A REFERENCE TO THE SNAGS THAT LIVE IN THE CINDER DEPRESSION.

take the Professor Winsnicker's Patented Grooming Comb and jab at the snag like mad. It may hurt a bit, but all good things come with a pinch—or in this case a repeated sting—of pain. If the snag persists, find some wooden shears and simply cut the offending hair out right above the problem area.

See how easy and fun looking nice can be? Combing yourself at least once every couple of days will make both your appearance and your life more enjoyable. You'll find yourself wanting to materialize much more often. You'll catch your reflection in a puddle or mirror and be surprised at how attractive I've helped you become.

Enough about hair.

I'm certain your parents have told you stories about when you were born. Good for them. I'm sure they talked about how cute you were and how happy they were when you arrived. In truth, they may have been happy, but I can tell you quite honestly, you

most definitely were not cute. Sorry, the truth smarts.

You see, every sycophant is born in a thin, stretchy sack that smells of sulfur and looks eerily like a moldy, deflated beach ball. If your parents were like most polite sycophants, they quickly slit open the sack, pulled you out, and threw the sack into the distance to save for another moment. They then probably fanned the air and tried to act like they couldn't smell anything. I have had the good fortune of attending a number of sycophant births, and let me just say, it takes some real acting to pull that off.

Then, after friends and family have come to see the brand-new baby, your mother sneaked off, retrieved the smelly sack, and, with the skill that only mothers possess, she fashioned it into the robe you are wearing today.

Take a moment to express the sentiment uppermost in your heart: *ewww.*

But don't fret. One of the most miraculous things about a sycophant is the robe you are essentially born with. If fashioned right, it can make you completely invisible from any eyes. And if cared for properly, it can last thousands and thousands of years. It is your most valuable possession. It, along with your secret, is what protects the entire race of sycophants and ultimately Foo.

HOW SYCOPHANTS DIE?

Wash it carefully.

Never take it off except to clean. Never borrow another's robe or alter it in any way. Only the one who has sewn the robe can make changes or repairs. If your mother has passed on, then you'd better be happy with the robe you have, because there isn't a soul in Foo who can change it.

Is CLOVER'S MOTHER STILL ALIVE?

Do not sell it, dye it, or iron it.

Do not gain so much weight that you outgrow it. Not to embarrass my own sycophant, Harold, but one summer a number of years back he ate a little more than he should have and his robe became a bit too tight for him. It was not without consequences. I never mentioned this to him, due to the fact that I am the model of decorum and good taste, but his robe became so tight that when he went invisible you could see bits of his left arm and an outline of his second chin. When he dropped the weight his robe began to work perfectly again.

Your robe is a part of you. Like your hair, you were born with it, and unless something incredibly awful or wrong happens within your lifetime, you will die with it. If it gets wet, let it dry. If it gets torn, find your mother. If it gets outdated, all you can do is hope that the style comes back around in another couple of hundred years.

Your robe is your responsibility. With it you can achieve amazing success. Clean hair and a nice robe make for the most marvelous of sycophants.

And I should know because, according to all the diplomas and plaques hanging on my wall, I am very, very smart.

ROOM FOR YOU TO REFLECT UPON WHAT I HAVE TAUGHT

Dear diary,

My name is Clover Ernest. I really like . . .

To whom it may concern,

My name is Clover Ernest. Professor Winsnicker just looked over my shoulder and informed me that I should not refer to my textbook as a diary. He also said that despite my inaccuracy I was a splendid-looking sycophant who he felt certain would blossom under his watchful eye. I then turned invisible and moved away from him. I think I'll make it a point to write things down when he is not around. I am now sitting on

the thick grass beneath a leafy orange
fantrum tree.

It is free period and we have been
granted time to reflect upon what we are
being taught. Professor Winsnicker seems very
smart. He certainly is a tall man with a high
forehead and a thick mustache that squirms
when he speaks. He wears an outdated brown
robe and thick black socks. He really has a
lot to say. I raised my hand earlier to ask
a question but he never answered it. He just
said he knew what I was going to say and
answered a completely different question than
I was planning to ask. I suppose I needed
the answer although I really just wanted to
know where the washroom was. *

*WAS HE
DISTRACTING
CLOVER ON PURPOSE?

I tried to comb my hair with one of the
combs he passed out, but I kept getting
distracted by a white sycophant two rows
up and three rows over. I don't know her

WINTER'S?

name, but it is obvious she knows how to
groom herself. I've never seen hair so shiny.
Her two ears are about
as lovely as any leaves
I have ever seen.

The lesson went pretty
well. I was a little sur-
prised to find out where
my robe came from. I
don't think I would
have been so bothered
if it had not been
for the fact that a couple
of years ago on a dare I tried to fit my
robe in my mouth. With the new knowledge
from today, my accomplishment seems less
cool and sort of gross.

I wish I could remember my birth, but like
all sycophants, I have completely forgotten
the first twenty years of my life. The air

from the Veil Sea has erased my early memories. I'm surprised my mother never gave away the secret of our robes. Knowing where my robe comes from makes me wonder what else I don't know and might be disgusted to find out.

I wanted to tell Professor Winsnicker about the addition my mother put on my robe, but I'm not sure it's something I should make public. Two days ago, on my seventy-third birthday, my mother sewed on a void. She said she had some extra robe material and she thought a sycophant like me might enjoy having a place to put all the interesting things I discover and pick up at school. I know now that the extra material was some sack saved from my birth. The void is very handy. So far I have put two long branches, a half dozen rocks, a bunch of candy, and a book about trees in it. Once

IS THERE MORE?

the things are placed into the void I can't
feel their weight or even tell they're there.
Maybe I'll inform the professor about it on
another day. I'm certain he'll have some extra
rules that I should be obeying because of it.

I want to become half the sycophant he
thinks I can be. I have always known that
sycophants were important, but so far all
I've learned is that we should look good
when we scare people. I hope he has more
to say. My mom seems to think that it is
going to take a lot of teaching to get me
ready to leave Sycophant Run. I don't . . .

Sorry if my handwriting is a bit shaky,
but the white sycophant just sat down on
the grass about three feet from me. She
smells like mint and seawater. She's practic-
ing her combing. It's glorious. She didn't look
directly at me, but it doesn't seem like she
is actually ignoring me either.

I'm going to comb myself extra well tonight.

I'm not very good at staying focused.

In fact, I'm not sure if I'll ever be ready to leave Sycophant Run, much less hunt and secure a burn of my own.

More later,

Clover

CHAPTER TWO

FINDING THE RIGHT BURN FOR YOU

Still with me? Excellent. Your life will be much better because of it. For the beginning of this chapter I am going to do something slightly different—I'm going to talk about myself for a bit. I know it is difficult to applaud while holding a book, so you are welcome to just cheer respectfully.

I grew up in a place called New York. It is a town in a state by the same name. My parents were Earl and Evelle Winsnicker. I had a brother named Winford and a sister named Tina. We had a nice brownstone home on Manhattan Island.

RESEARCH SHOWS THAT HIS FATHER, EARL, WAS A POLITICIAN.

New York City

I had a dog named Harold, and my brother had a parrot named Flinch. I grew up with the best of education and upbringing. On more than two occasions I have personally heard people say, "My, my, if Philip Winsnicker isn't socially impressive."

I would blush, but honesty does not embarrass me.

In Reality I was studying to be a great teacher at the impressive Yale University when fate snatched me and brought me to Foo. I can still remember the occasion. I was walking across campus holding a fantastic collection of intellectual books. It was late and the library had just closed. I paused for a brief moment right above the spot where Elm Street and *York Street meet.* Apparently there was some unevenness in the junction because as I looked up to witness a shooting star in the warm night air I was suddenly snapped up by Foo, leaving nothing but an impressive selection of books lying piled on the ground.

* I HAVE SEEN THE UNEVEN GAP.

All that remains of Professor Winsnicker in Reality.

I arrived in Foo about a mile north, or up, from Morfit. In an instant all I knew was gone. I thought I was dreaming, or sick, but I could tell that what I was looking at was, in a sense, real. I could see the dark hull of Morfit standing in front of me like a mountainous nightmare.

Before I could even assess what had happened, I was suddenly under attack by hundreds of sycophants. They appeared out of nowhere, jumping on me and promising me protection and adjustment. They told me things I was well aware of—things about how smart I was and how I should be wise and pick them personally. Some sycophants stroked my hair; others clung to my leg begging to be chosen.

Well, I swatted at them for a number of minutes before a nice-looking red one in a white robe pushed off all the others and won me over. His name was Reed, but I changed it to Harold in honor of our family dog. Harold has been a faithful and dedicated sycophant ever since. And, at the risk of embarrassing him, I must say that I think I have really helped make his life complete.

For those whom fate steals away to Foo, there is nothing as wonderful as a sycophant. I can't imagine how I ever got along without one in Reality. And for the sycophant, there is nothing more natural or fulfilling than finding and serving a burn. We call them burns because you as sycophants literally burn for them. You feel great motivation and desire to serve and comfort them. It is a burning within that creates the magnificent bond between you and the nit you end up with, whoever that may be.

Of course, not everyone can be as fortunate as Harold. In the lottery of life he has done quite well to land me.

When the time comes, you will begin your hunt for your first burn. You must listen to the wind and read the stars. You must follow the instinct that fate has set in you. The first twenty years of your life

NO MENTION OF AVOIDING THE HISSING OF SOIL

HAROLD

were filled with lessons that the Veil Sea has now wiped from your memory. Those lessons, however, lie still in your soul waiting for your instinct to awaken them.

I HAVE NOT FOUND WHAT CAUSES THIS.

Fate wants you to discover what you know on your own.

You will begin to be drawn to spots in Foo that are the right places for you to settle in and wait. You will recognize things in the nature of your surroundings that will help you know just where and how soon fate will pull in its newest recruits. Unlike so many other things, I can't do this one for you. Finding the right burn will take patience, intuition, and moxie. But I have never known a persistent sycophant who has not eventually ended up with a burn.

Let me add, the act of obtaining a burn is not a contest. Yes, Harold is lucky to have landed me, but this is not about one-upping each other. So you end up being the burn for Al Capone, who was a notorious criminal in Reality—that's no more prestigious than hooking up with, say, Jim Broadmiller, who sold shoes. I have witnessed many a sycophant pass up a terrific burn in hopes of getting someone more important, mysterious, or attractive.

When it comes to burns, heed my advice and take what fate lines up for you. Finding the right burn is a matter of simply making yourself open and available. With fate as your guide, you will do splendidly.

Someone is out there.

Someone is coming. It is not up to you to decide if who you burn for is right. It is up to you to make sure whoever you burn for is happy and well-adjusted.

The sycophant's role since the beginning of time has always been to soothe the troubled souls who wander into Foo. Make them feel at home and help them discover and cultivate their nit gift. Every human being who is snatched into Foo is special and worthy of your attention.

For now, just try not to envy Harold. Rather, look forward to the day when you will have your own less-educated burn.

I'VE GIVEN YOU MUCH TO CHEW ON. WRITE AWAY.

To whom it may concern,

School's not quite as much fun as I thought it would be. Today we were told that we can't be picky about who we burn for. So my dream about my burn having auburn hair and a big smile is over.

I know I shouldn't complain, but sometimes I feel like I'm just not cut out to be a sycophant.

My _father_ has always begged me to be more like my perfect brothers and sisters. They can think of nothing else besides the day they get their first burn. I try sometimes to be good, but there are just so many things to distract me. I'm certain that a sycophant with my failings will be stuck

IS HE STILL ALIVE? YES!

with the most undesirable burn around. I'll probably end up with a really old man who insists that the only way he can adjust to Foo is to have his wrinkled feet massaged daily.

Sometimes I wish I wasn't a sycophant.

I should probably erase that last line. I just don't want to fight a bunch of sycophants only to claim the prize of being able to serve some human who makes me do his chores. I know most sycophants would love just such a thing, but me, I think it's stupid.

If I had my choice I would <u>work with the</u> <u>Eggmen</u> beneath the Devil's Spiral making candy. That's a future. I've already had two really good ideas for treats. One is a cookie that works as a Frisbee. That way you could toss it around with a friend and take a bite each time you catch it.

THIS IS NO SURPRISE.

My *second idea* is a peppermint *stick*
with a timer on it. It would force the licker
to finish in a certain amount of time before
the candy stick exploded into a thousand
little sugary shards.

If I worked for the
Eggmen I could spend my days
coming up with ideas and watching the water
shoot through the Devil's Spiral and up in   ONE OF
the sky.   MY FAVORITE
                                                 SITES AS WELL

Instead I'm stuck waiting for a burn to
give me purpose.

My mother never had a burn, and she is
happy. There has to be a way for me to get

out of it. I could fake an illness, but I'd have to fake it for too many years. I could run away, but then I could never come back.

I know I should just trust in fate. I guess I could find a burn who will change my life and make me complete. Someone who makes me feel like the white sycophant makes me feel . . . the white sycophant who, by the way, just sat down across the field from me. I still don't know her name, but I think I heard someone call her Filly.

Filly is the most beautiful name I've ever heard.

Hold on a moment . . . a tall sycophant with a strip of black hair down the back of his head is walking right up to her.

He's waving at her.

She's waving back at him.

He's talking to her and she's smiling. He

just called her Lilly, and now he has
disappeared.

OF
COURSE!

  Lilly?

  I was wrong. Lilly is the most beautiful
name I have ever heard. Lilly. ♡

  She's eating a bickerwick and has her
legs crossed at the ankles. I wonder who her
lucky burn will be?

  Professor Winsnicker just came out of the
school building and is calling us to gather
around him so he can tell us about something impressive he just thought of.

  Much more later,

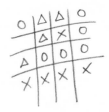

Chapter Three

Staying Invisible and Out of the Way

My goodness, it is hot. As I pen this chapter it is midsummer in Foo and warmer than I ever remember it being.* The fantrum trees outside of my cozy cottage are gasping for breath and shedding leaves in an effort to cool themselves. I will make it a point to hose them down a bit later. For now the bicker-wicks are feasting off the sweat of the trees.

It is so warm that Harold has been spending most of his time wiping off my sweaty brow. I try not to complain too much about the heat, knowing how Harold enjoys toweling me down.

*DOES THE TEMPERATURE IN FOO AFFECT THOSE WHO ARE SNATCHED IN?

I love to give.

Speaking of others, how are you doing? I know I have tossed you right into a deep pool of knowledge and facts. Swim, my young friend, swim! Yes, it is a lot to take in, but once you make it a part of your life, you will discover that my tips and tricks are not only invaluable, they are brilliant.

Most people and creatures both here and in Reality are better off when they take a moment to listen to those who know more than they do. This is a principle and point I have tried to teach others for many years.

So please, listen up.

We are now going to talk about a very important aspect of being a sycophant: invisibility.

If it were not for your robe and the incredible gift you have of fading in and out, you would be no better than the tharms of the Swollen Forest. One could argue that you would smell better, having higher standards of hygiene, but aside from that you would be far from special and somewhat ordinary in

THREE ARMS

Foo. Without your gift of invisibility, Sycophant Run would be just another piece of land. You, my dear friend, are who you are largely because of whom you can hide from.

Invisible.

There is an old school of thought that suggests, "A sycophant should not be seen or heard." But Foo has grown a bit more progressive, and I personally think Harold is worth talking to and looking at. I

Invisible Sycophant

know he instinctually burns for me regardless, but I do make it a point to appreciate and acknowledge him as often as is appropriate. Most worthwhile sycophant-nit relationships are ones in which the sycophant shows himself just enough but not too much—a delicate balance, to be sure, but one that is achievable by anyone willing to give it the time and effort.

When I stepped into Foo and sycophants fought over me, I was quite frightened. Then, after Harold won, I was still unnerved. It was at this point that Harold had the good sense to fade out and to speak to me primarily in short, comforting sentences. Here are three he used most often:

"It's going to be all right."

"You're in Foo, and you're fine."

"Close your mouth, your breath stinks."

For the record, stress makes my stomach sour.* And I am man enough to admit that being snatched from Reality into Foo can be a tad stressful. The important thing to remember is that I *am* man

* I HAVE HEARD OTHERS JOKE ABOUT THIS VERY FACT.

enough, and that Harold was wise enough to stay invisible as he comforted me. Eventually, I longed to see who was speaking to me, and when he showed himself I was in a better frame of mind and more able to take it all in.

It was many weeks before I was comfortable enough to have Harold materialize for long periods of time. He slowly introduced himself so that it would feel natural. As soon as I was comfortable with him, he began to share helpful tidbits of knowl-edge and to instruct me. He started to compliment me on things I was good at in hopes of helping me develop my nit gift. He was the first to notice how strong and solid my eyesight was, and the first to suggest that perhaps my gift was seeing through stone. ONE OF THE WEAKER GIFTS.

He was right.

Harold then began to point out incoming dreams. It took me a full year to clearly spot my first one, but when I did, Harold pushed me inside of it and whispered what I should do.

Professor Winsnicker demonstrates his special gift.

Sycophants are very necessary to Foo.

Don't get too impressed with yourself, however. No one likes an egotistical sycophant. The point is that you, as a sycophant, are in control. You hold the power to help in the proper adjustment process for those whom fate has snatched. Your instinct will let you know for whom you should burn, and that instinct, combined with my instruction, will help you know how to be the most appropriate and effective sycophant possible.

For most occasions you will find that staying invisible is to your advantage. There are small conveniences like being able to blush in private, but your invisibility also protects you from those who might wish to do you harm. It also lets those with whom your burn interacts focus on your burn and not on you. It is a naughty, spiteful sycophant who tries to steal any attention for himself or herself.

It is fate that will put you in the hands of your burn; let fate be the one who dictates his or her decisions. Let fate chart your nit's course. You are there to comfort, tend, and lighten the load. Show yourself only when it is wise and selfless. It is not that we object to having you around; we simply don't wish to be shown up.

Take, for example, the time Harold materialized and answered a question one of the Council of Whisps had asked me directly. There have been only a few moments of strain in my relationship with Harold, but I must say that was one of the most strenuous moments. I hate to dig up old dirt, but for the sake of your learning, I'll recount the story.

You see, it was years ago, and a council member had just assigned me to travel to Cusp and instruct the nits there on the importance of manipulating and not dominating dreams.

This council member had then asked me, "Is this something you feel you can do, Professor?"

Well, Harold, without thinking, leapt in and answered, "Professor Winsnicker can do anything."

Although Harold was merely speaking the truth, it was still uncomfortable for me to have my sycophant answering my question. Of course, I handled the situation with tact and diplomacy by making a small joke about how Harold has such a hard time holding back the compliments. But even though I made things right, it was still inappropriate.

Stay hidden. Hold your thoughts. You are there to comfort and guide. Here is a little poem I made up to help you remember this:

> If wondering when to be seen,
> Take this tip to heart:
> Your place is not to show and tell
> But to quietly play your part.

I did pen additional verses and even put them to music, but I feel for now that this simple and concise first verse is plenty. What's important is that you remember to stay hidden. This is not only the best thing for your burn, it is also the safest thing for you.

And that, my dear friend, is my very highest concern.

TAKE COPIOUS NOTES—I HAVE SAID A LOT OF IMPORTANT THINGS.

Dearest Journal,

I am learning so much. Professor Winsnicker is so smart. (At least that's what the plaque he gave me says.) Right now we are working on the importance of invisibility. This is a hard thing for me. I must admit, I enjoy having others see me. I feel my personality is better understood if you can see my expressions and hand gestures while I'm talking. I told Professor Winsnicker that, and he said that I had better change my ways or life would be nothing but thorns and dirt and filthy laundry. I could tell he was sort of drifting and couldn't find the words he actually wanted to use to scold me.

Two classmates left today in search of

burns. Professor Winsnicker called their departure premature and shortsighted. He told a long story about how those two sycophants would live less fulfilling lives because they would not be _privy_ to the vast amounts of information he had yet to divulge. He then instructed us all to feel very, very sorry for the two of them.

I confess, I don't feel that sorry. Sure, they are each going to be stuck with a burn, but at least they are on their own. Every day I stare out the window of our classroom and wish I was looking for leaves or sticks or Lilly. I talked to her for the first time the other day. She was combing her hair and reciting Professor Winsnicker's poem when I stepped up to her and said, I'm not sure if I'm shedding.

It wasn't what I had meant to say, but, seeing it combined with my facial

CLOVER'S VOCABULARY WAS MUCH MORE PROPER BEFORE HIS TIME IN REALITY.

expressions and hand gestures, she seemed to get it. Of course, two seconds later she disappeared.

Lilly.

I know that someday I will get a burn and that perhaps I can turn out to be a great sycophant. I think maybe then Lilly will be able to stop looking at other sycophants and fall in love with me. At the moment I can think of no other reason for me to seek out a burn than to win her over.

I found a pamphlet the other day with pictures and ads for the latest candies the Eggmen are making. I thought it was fate that the pamphlet just fell into my hands, but then I remembered that I had actually snuck into the study room, opened Professor Winsnicker's top desk drawer, and rummaged through his supplies and papers until I found it.

I'm not a very good sycophant.

Still, it must have been some sort of fate for me to have found the candy pamphlet in his desk. I have read and stared at the pictures and descriptions so many times I can quote them from memory:

Caramel Thickets are a delicious and highly protective candy. Suppose, for instance, you are being pursued by a vicious pack of rovens who wish to sell you to the sarus. Simply place one delicious Caramel Thicket in your mouth, and in moments your finger-nails, teeth, and toenails will grow so rapidly, and in so many different and sticky directions, that you will be encased in a nice thicket of your own making. Take two

THESE ARE DELICIOUS BUT <u>MESSY</u>!

pieces and no one will ever be able to get to you.

I should have been born an egg. It's a good thing you can't see my expression now. You might become as discouraged as I am.

Until next time,

Clover Ernest

Sycophant in Training

CHAPTER FOUR

FEEL FREE TO SKIP THIS CHAPTER

Did you know that during my first thirty years in Foo I received six different awards for various achievements? I mention this only so you may be even more enthused and excited to be sitting there learning directly from me.

One of the awards I won was in Morfit, for clapping longer than anyone else after the Sochemists announced that the general tone of dreams seemed to be more hopeful than it was a few years back. I clapped for two straight days. I was not only happy about the news but felt that in some small selfless

CONFUSED
&
BOTHERSOME

and unrecognized way I had contributed to the happy occasion through the stirring and informative teaching I had done while in Cusp.

Awards are funny things. It is embarrassing to be singled out, and yet I have always felt a civic responsibility to let my neighbors know so that they could calculate the extra value of their property that would come from living near someone such as I.

Let me tell you a story one such neighbor told me. Once, there was a certain person in Foo who had the worst time picking out the color of paint to use in painting his home. He looked at sample after sample: first blue, then green, then orange, then pink, then red, then brown, then yellow, then smarm, then white, then black. He then got a brush with short hair, a brush with long hair, a brush with medium hair, a brush with roven hair, a brush with . . .

. . . are you still with me? Sorry about that incredibly boring story, but what I have to share with you next is so important that I needed to hide it a bit. And I knew that if I stuck it in between things

I had said, everyone would be riveted and just keep reading, and then it wouldn't be a secret to anyone.

What we need to talk about right now is your bite.

Now, like the origin of your robe, the power of your bite might come as a surprise to you. Certainly, sycophants are here to serve, and yes, you are to help create a Foo where strong, wonderful dreams can flourish. But fate knew before you did that there would be days and weeks when you simply needed a break.

Thus the gift of your bite.

Hopefully you are aware of your teeth. Most likely you have used them to chew and eat. That is good. It is entirely possible to choke if you swallow food too big to fit down your throat. But your teeth are much more than you might have imagined. In fact, there have been few sets of choppers as miraculous throughout the dawn of time.

You, my young, magnificent friend, have within you the gift to put anyone into a wonderful trance.

This gift should be used only on your burn.

All you need do is bite down on any fleshy part of your burn and then shake your head. Your teeth will release a liquid that will knock out even the tallest and fattest nit. I've seen a three-hundred-pound nit drop like a sack of claws after being bitten by a six-inch sycophant.

The purpose of such a bite is to put your burn in a state of sycophantic bliss. Your burn can then lie there for quite some time without suffering any damage. While in the trance, he or she will see nothing but wonderful images and visions about the glory and grandeur of sycophants. So, when you wake your burn after enjoying some much needed "me time," he or she will be not only unaware of having ever been out but revived and greatly enthused about you and your breed.*

It is a wonderful ability.

All sycophants grow weary of their burns at one time or another. And a short-term break is often a long-term solution. Actually, I shouldn't pen that

* CLOVER BIT LEVEN MORE THAN ONCE.

Harold demonstrates perfecting your bite.

all sycophants grow weary of their burns. I know, for example, that Harold has never bitten me.

From what I have studied, it seems you can bite at any fleshy exposure, but the best place to sink your teeth into your burn is where the back of the neck meets the back of the shoulder. Then, with a simple shake of your head, your burn will be dreaming of you almost instantly.

You might experiment first on a piece of fruit or a fat bickerwick. There is some art in the biting and shaking, but it is a natural thing for you and should come easily.

After your burn has been out for a long enough time, you must revive him or her. To do so, simply whisper into the person's right ear these five words:

Arise and dream of Foo

Only you can awaken your burn from the trance you have induced. There is something about the combination of words and the familiarity of your voice that pulls your burn out.

IT HAS TO BE THESE FIVE WORDS EXACTLY.

There is also some caution to be upheld concerning the length of time you leave your burn out. If left asleep for too long, burns will begin to lose bits and portions of their brains and will awake considerably different nits from who they once were. Usually no more than a few days to a week is recommended. I have known some people to recover fine after three weeks in a trance, but it can be risky.

Take care, my great pupils. Use this gift wisely . . .

. . . so my neighbor ended up painting the entire place a dull shade of yellow. And when his friends came to visit they would say, "What a nice job you did." "What a nice color." "What a lot of work you've put into the place." "What a good choice." And he lived happily ever after.

I hope you enjoyed this story my neighbor once told me. As for myself, I found it dull.

Clovery

REGARDLESS, YOU SHOULD TAKE SOME NOTES.

Dear Journal,

I take it all back. I like school. Not only did I get to learn about our gift of knocking burns out, but today while Professor Winsnicker was going on about our ability to bite, he mentioned that Harold had never bitten him. He then pointed at Harold and asked him if this wasn't the case. Harold blushed so brightly the entire room lit up. Professor Winsnicker then sputtered and coughed, demanding that Harold tell him the truth. Eventually Harold admitted to having bitten Professor Winsnicker over one hundred times.

Well, the professor began to sob. Harold tried to console him, but it was no use. After crying for ten minutes, Professor

Winsnicker announced that there would be a
 new chapter in our books called, When
Sycophants Go Bad. Harold started to cry.
Then the class started to cry, thinking the
new chapter would be filled with extra work.
And the <u>chairs at our desks folded into</u>
<u>themselves</u> in protest at possibly having to
hold us up for additional class periods.

    A really fat sycophant at the front of
the class threw his pencil at the professor,
and soon the air was filled with whatever
anyone could find to throw.

I'VE HEARD THAT
CHAIRS CAN BE QUITE
TEMPERAMENTAL.

    Eventually Professor Winsnicker announced
that there would be a two-week break for us
all to spend thinking about what Harold had

done and how wrong that was. He then stormed out, with Harold groveling behind him.

It was the best lesson we've had yet.

Not only that, but now that I know about our bite, being a sycophant doesn't seem that awful. If I can simply bite my burn anytime I need to get out, I think I can make this work.

I can't wait for school to start back up.

I've got to go now. I need to see if I can find some fruit to practice on.

That's it,

METAL AND SHINY OBJECTS: WHAT NOT TO TOUCH

Here we are in chapter five already. How exciting! Think of all the things you now know that you didn't know such a short time ago. I wish I could shake every one of your hands and accept your gratitude personally, but time is knowledge, and we must get on.

If reviewers somewhere were to critique this textbook, they would be hard-pressed to find things to complain about. But I must admit that I have one weakness, and that is in being too generous. Others might read this book and say, "Insightful." "Brilliant."

I WONDER...

57

I have known many sycophants who have put
themselves in dangerous situations by letting themselves
be distracted by the shine of metal.

"Couldn't put it down." But in the back of their minds they might be thinking, "Professor Winsnicker is overly kind and complimentary about the sycophants."

For that I apologize. But you are an important breed being taught by a great teacher.

If pressed, however, I think I could find a thing or two that would show you to be vulnerable and less than perfect. For example, most sycophants are too easily distracted by shiny metal objects.

How many times have nits suffered sprained ankles or bumps on the noggin due to their sycophants being too distracted to warn them of chuckholes in the road or low-hanging tree branches?

A truly great sycophant is not easily distracted and is always aware of what his or her burn needs.

It is a fact of Foo that, at present, metal is forbidden. Metal only leads to the building of destructive and awful things. But there was a time in Foo when metal was worked with freely—a time less civilized than now. As we became more enlightened, we began to understand how dangerous and wrong metal could be. We have since spent many years burying and destroying everything that was ever made of metal. Most of it, thanks to the rovens, is buried deep beneath the surface, but on occasion bits and pieces poke up. And I am saddened to say that it seems as if the sycophants are the first to notice and the first to be drawn to those fragments.

Let me make this clear:

Do not touch anything metal.

It will lead to no good. ~~Harold~~, my sycophant, knows how dangerous it can be. Once a school chum of his found a metal blade and accidentally cut off his own big toe. Due to the carelessness of his friend, ~~Harold~~ learned a valuable lesson that day.

Do not touch anything metal.

If the Council of Whisps or the Council of Wonder were to hear that sycophants were digging up metal objects, they would most certainly bring it to the attention of the Want. And who knows what the Want would do to you and your breed.

*SO THE ROVENS ONCE WORKED FOR G...

Do not touch anything metal.

You will be curious. It will be hard for you to keep your hands off shiny metal objects, should you happen to encounter them. Focus instead on rocks that glow and glass that shines. Their allure is far less blinding.

These things are perfectly acceptable for you to touch and hold.

But whatever you do, do not touch anything metal.

I cannot stress enough how important this lesson is. Do not go near anything or anyone who is holding something that is made of metal. I have known many sycophants who have put themselves in dangerous situations by letting themselves be distracted by the shine of metal.

I apologize for the stern tone and inflections I have used throughout this chapter. Life in Foo is not always rosy. Sometimes it takes a great man to speak up and articulate how things are. I hope you can see clearly that I am that great man, and this is how things are.

Do not touch anything metal.

YOU ARE FREE NOW TO EXPRESS YOURSELF. FREE EXPRESSION IS OFTEN BEST IF IT REVOLVES AROUND MY TEACHINGS.

Dear Journal,

Our first day back at school Professor Winsnicker was in a less than glowing mood. He started off by telling us that he had worked on a short lesson for his proposed chapter on When Sycophants Go Bad, but in the end his humble and giving attitude prevailed and he just couldn't create an entire chapter about how awful Harold could be. He also admitted that he was the one who had gone through all of our books and crossed out Harold's name in this last chapter. He then stood in front of the class and insisted that he was no longer upset, and that to show how gracious he was, he was going to

allow Harold to bite him so the class could
see how it worked. He instructed Harold to
wake him up a few seconds later.

Harold gladly bit him, but under pressure
from the rest of us he didn't wake the
professor up for another two weeks, during
which time we learned nothing. Harold tried to
teach the chapter on not touching metal, but
we weren't paying as much attention as we
should have. We all went outside every
day and did whatever we wanted. I
built a fort out of long, dry fantrum
branches. Lilly was the first one I invited
to come in, but she declined, claiming she
was too busy doing nothing. Her face
is so beautiful when she makes
excuses.

When Harold finally woke Professor
Winsnicker up, the poor guy had no clue how
long he had been out. He just smiled and

complained about being hungry, at which point he dismissed the class for lunch and instructed us to write in our textbooks.

All in all, it's been a pretty good stretch of school. It's also comforting to know that when things get hard, we can pressure Harold into biting the professor for us.

I'm not feeling like the greatest sycophant at the moment.

Oh, well,

Clover not always Ernest

WHAT A SHAME THAT IT WAS THIS CHAPTER THEY WERE SHORTED ON.

When Sycophants
Go Bad

I will try not to let my disappointment show
as I pen this new, spontaneous chapter.

First off, let me say that I am so disappointed
not only in Harold but in sycophants in general. Yes, I have given most of the years of
my life in Foo to them; yes, I have gone above
and beyond the call of duty in trying to make
sycophants an even greater presence; yes, I
am one of the very few nits who has ever
been allowed to travel to Sycophant Run; and
yes, I am educated in numerous important
and impressive things, but despite all that I
am, I am still disappointed.

I extended trust, and Harold bit the neck that led him.

It is because of Harold's poor judgment that I have decided to write this additional chapter. Here are ten things I think sycophants and particularly Harold should do better:

1. Don't bite nits who don't need it.

2. Don't do things that betray your burn.

3. Don't secretly hurt those who care for you.

4. Stop making decisions on your own.

5. Better recognize genius.

6. Don't announce to small gatherings how you bit your burn hundreds of times.

7. Don't forget that one of the six awards I have won was for helping you, Harold.

8. Be gracious.

9. *Stop crying, I'll forgive you.*

10. *Making a warm mug of chocolate and rubbing feet is an appropriate way to say I'm sorry.*

There is nothing uglier than a sycophant who oversteps his or her boundaries. I was tempted to make up long charts and extra work for you sycophants to do, but I smell chocolate and feel that I need to be the bigger man and prepare myself to accept Harold's apology. Thus this chapter will never see the light of day. I feel wasteful destroying anything I have written, so I'll carefully hide it somewhere no one can find it. I would hate to have Harold discover it and feel awkward about the figurative milk he spilt.

HE FAILED IN THAT RESPECT.

Clov   CLov

CHAPTER SIX
DEALING WITH NAME CHANGES

How nice. Here we are almost halfway through your course. I am sure your esteem and confidence are growing rapidly. Good for you. You are obviously on your way to becoming a fine graduate. You have had a lot of education in your life, but none of it is as important or as timely as the facts and figures you are now learning from me.

I BELIEVE HE'S REFERRING TO THEIR PREP SCHOOLS.

There is still much lecturing ahead, but do not despair. If ever you get to feeling that I am simply filling your head with too much knowledge, just think of the fantastic-looking certificate with my

CLOVER

(name)

was lucky enough to be taught
at the feet of the
actual Professor Philip Winsnicker.

Professor Philip Winsnicker

signature on it that you will earn at the course's completion.

During my first years in Foo there was so much to see and understand, despite the piles of things I already saw and understood.

Like so many who are snatched into Foo, I wandered the landscape looking for something to help make sense of it all. I believe that even with my steady and learned mind, I might not have made it if it had not been for my beloved Harold. He was such a comfort—saying nice things, assuring me. I also found it to be a salve that his name was Harold. Yes, when we first met his name was Reed, but his accepting my change made my state of mind so much better. Harold was the name of our family dog, and now I had a new friend with the same name.

It comforted me.

I'm not sure I could have been comforted by a Reed. Not only does it sound like a last name, but it reminds me of Mark Reed, a tall boy who used

to pummel me with his fists on my school play-
ground in Reality.

Where's the comfort in that?

Thanks to Harold being a good sycophant and
having no problem with me changing his name, I
was able to cope better.

Yes, you have a name now, but be prepared to
change it. Don't grow too attached to what your parents labeled you. Most sycophants are named after
things of nature simply because their parents didn't
want to put too much thought into a name when
they knew it would probably change someday.

CLOVER, I'VE DISCOVERED, WAS ACTUALLY A FAMILY NAME.

This name change can often be frightening to a
sycophant. Do not worry. It is painless and ultimately exciting. And it will probably happen more
than once or twice in your lifetime. It is not uncom-
mon for sycophants to have multiple burns. If your
burn rejects you or passes on, you may, as do many
sycophants, seek to find a new burn. With that new
burn often comes a new name.

MOST NITS & COGS LIVE ABOUT 150 YEARS.

It is not up to you to debate this practice. As a

sycophant you must simply accept the new moniker and move on.

For the most part, nits are pretty fair about what they choose to call you. Usually the name they pick is something familiar or meaningful to them. They might name you after a sister or a brother or someone they admired. On rare occasions you might find a nit that is cruel and simply wants to name you something that will express his or her confusion and bitterness at being snatched from Reality. I have met a sycophant named Mudwadd.

That's just unfortunate.

The important thing to remember is that whether you are Mudwadd or Harold, your purpose is to make your burn comfortable. And when the time comes that your burn passes on it is perfectly acceptable to revert back to your old name, although it is not required. I know, for instance, that Harold would never change back to Reed. Many sycophants find their new names much more charming and well thought out.

CLOVER

Once you have your new name, it might be a good idea to practice saying it over and over. Pretend you are in a crowded street market and someone is yelling at you from across the way. Do you recognize your new name? If not, yell it at yourself a few hundred times. I have found that it helps to write yourself letters and cards wishing your new name well. Buy a belt and get your name burned into the leather. All these things help you to become your new self.

So, my soon-to-be-new-named friend, do not be afraid. Someday people will call you something other than what they call you now, and when they do, it will feel perfectly natural and acceptable.

For now, all that matters is that I call you my pupil.

LET'S PAUSE TO SORT OUT OUR FEELINGS.

Dear Mr. Feldstein M. Journal,

There, how do you like that? I changed my journal's name. I'm not sure how I feel about having someone I've not yet met tinkering around with my name. I have always thought Clover sounded neat. I can't think of anything worse than being named Parnellithan or Trumpador. Professor Winsnicker says I don't need to worry about being named either of those, seeing as how they're made-up names that nobody would give me, but I still think my point is clear. Who knows what they'll give me?

What if they mistake me for a girl and name me something flowery? What if the only thing that comforted them in Reality was litter, so they name me Waste? Once again it

THIS CLEARS THINGS UP.
I DISCOVERED A POSTCARD MADE OUT TO
STEVEN Q. BOTWORTHY. IT MUST HAVE BEEN
TO CLOVER FROM CLOVER.

seems as if we sycophants get the short end of the stick.

I suppose if I could change it to what I liked, that would be different. I wouldn't mind being called Ted. Or Barry. Or Steven Q. Botworthy. Hopefully I will get a burn who lets me give some input.

As scary as it is to think of having my named changed, I think it would be even worse to see Lilly get relabeled. What if she became Clodsdell or Spitsmick? Again, Professor Winsnicker pointed out that Lilly would probably never be called those things because they are nonsense. And Lilly added that she would prefer I not wonder about her name change.

I think she is warming up to me.

Professor Winsnicker has been a little down lately. At first we thought he was still mad at Harold, but I think it is actually

because more and more dreams coming into
Foo are worrying him. He says the Want is
growing irritable, and that we as sycophants
can help make things better. He says that
as we help nits adjust and master their
gifts, we can also encourage them to manipulate dreams in a way that will make both
Reality and Foo better and healthier.

I guess I need to think about that a bit.

Steven Q. Botworthy

lunch...

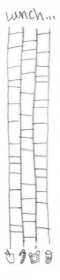

Chapter Seven

Making Your Burn Feel at Home

This is a very important chapter—very, very, important.

If I were to rank it, I would place it high enough to be published in a book as prestigious as the one you are now holding. Well, what do you know? It already has been!

I've got a terrific sense of humor.

I'll stop pointing out the obvious and get on with it. To those whom fate snatches and brings into Foo, this place can be extremely scary and confusing. Imagine living and working in one place and the next second finding yourself in a completely new realm

77

hidden within the folds of your own mind. Imagine seeing the Swollen Forest or the Veil Sea for the first time. Imagine if everyone you loved or cared about or even had a tough time with was suddenly out of your life. That cousin you hated? Gone. Your parents? Gone. That loud dog that never sleeps? Gone. Everything you ever knew? Gone.

I SHOULD LOOK INTO THIS.

Those who are snatched here from Reality do not always adjust easily.

It might be hard for you to understand this, seeing how well-adjusted I am despite having been taken from Reality. But the truth is, nits need you to make them feel at home. This requires extra effort and a healthy amount of studying from you.

You never know where your burn might come from. Russia? Africa? America? China?

The better you know the geography and layout of Reality, the better sycophant you will be. Language should not be a problem, as no matter what you speak, Foo sorts it out. But knowing a

The better you know the geography of Reality,
the better sycophant you will be.

few cultures and customs can go a long way toward helping your burn adjust.

I remember feeling particularly blue a few months after I arrived here. Harold had explained to me about dreams and how important it would be for me to help enhance dreams that came in. I felt the responsibility weighing heavily on my shoulders. I missed Reality and all the many things I used to do and see. I missed those I loved and those I had not had the time to teach and instruct. I missed New York and my home. I'm not the sort of person to wallow in pity, but I allowed myself a few moments to wade around in my much-deserved misery.

Well, Harold, being the exceptional sycophant that he is, found some fabric and stitched me a New York Yankees baseball shirt. True, he spelled *New York* wrong, but his intention made me feel worlds better and helped me realize that there were plenty of souls for me to teach and instruct here in Foo.

On another occasion Harold made me what he thought was a traditional New York meal. It was

actually a sausage wrapped in a piece of splotch, covered in pickled mash, with the words *New York* spelled out in mustard across the top, but I did an above-average job of pretending to enjoy it.

MUCH LIKE HEAVY BREAD.

I remember even making a joke about how my mother had never made a meal so tasty.

Again with the sense of humor.

Perhaps the best way for you to become familiar with and make your burn feel comfortable is to read. Read all you can get your hands on. Read books with tattered covers and broken spines. Read new books that no one has touched before and books that have markings in the margins. Read books that look hard and books that appear simple. Just read. Read pamphlets and epic novels. Read history books and journals. Read a little on some days, a lot on others, and often in between. Read books with odd book jackets and books that wear no jackets at all.

Read books about cooking and books about eating. Read about animals you can't stand and people you can. Read in the dark with a tiny light or in the

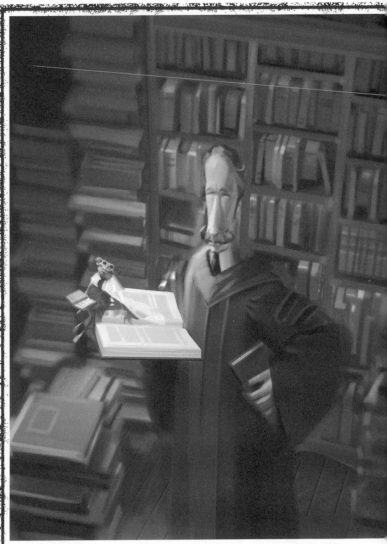

Professor Winsnicker sets the example of reading excellence.

middle of the field with the noonday sun shining all around you. Read before bed, after breakfast, and in between conversations. Read while you are standing still or running swiftly from a bothersome avaland.

Just read.

The more information your head holds, the better equipped you will be to make your burn feel at home. Suppose, for example, your burn mentions a "yo-yo." A less-educated sycophant might think that the burn has misspoken and is actually talking about a "Yo-you," which we all know is a handy, ball-like object that you can throw at someone across the room and it will attach to that person and try to get his or her attention for you. But a Yo-you is not what your burn is actually referencing.

Think how nice it would be if you were well-read and had already finished the terrific book* *Toby Finds Something in the Mesh Pocket of His Backpack:* "A simple story of friendship between a boy named Toby and his yo-yo." You would know that a yo-yo is

*I TRIED TO CHECK THIS BOOK OUT, BUT IT HAD BEEN TAKEN FROM THE LIBRARY AND NEVER RETURNED.

actually a toy disk that you spin up and down on a string.

Information is power.

As you read, you will begin to know of so many things your burn might bring up. Nothing is more comforting for the newly snatched than knowing they have someone with whom to share common knowledge.

You alone can be a bit scary and unsettling—sorry if that sounds harsh. But you with an added dash of meaningful cultural knowledge can be so much more comforting and helpful. It is the sacred duty of sycophants to make their burns feel comfortable, to help them discover their gifts, and to teach them to manipulate dreams. In a sense, the fate of mankind depends upon you reading.

Get to it.

Of course, as usual, it would be wise to write down a few thoughts about what I have said first.

To whom it may concern,

I don't know what's wrong with me. I've been sweating a lot lately and feeling more jumpy than usual. The other day I found myself inadvertently running as if toward something. When I stopped, I was miles away from home and completely baffled by my own behavior. I asked Professor Winsnicker what might be happening to me and he simply smiled and said I was tiptoeing around the fruits of my first burn.

Sometimes I don't think he's quite as smart as he tells us he is.

His latest lesson started off annoying me: Making our burns happy. I didn't think I would want to spend my days doing nothing but helping someone else. But as his lesson went on and on, it began to make sense. I started to sweat and feel as if there was somewhere else I needed to be. I could even see a (young person) in my head who I don't believe I've ever seen or dreamed about before.

LEVEN?

By the time Professor Winsnicker pulled out and put on the shirt Harold had made for him, I couldn't stop thinking about making a shirt for my own burn someday.

I asked Professor Winsnicker if it was normal for sycophants to see people in their heads. He said it was not at all unusual for sycophants to think back fondly to the days when they had been taught things by him. He then added that only the most fateful of burns appear in the heads of sycophants before they appear in Foo.

I'm confused. And sweaty.

Lilly is resting on a large rock about thirty feet away from me. She appears to be reading a book.

I bet her head is crammed with all kinds of wonderful things. When she reads, the hair on her forearms bristles. It's amazing. How lucky her burn will be. It makes me almost want to be a nit to get the chance to have her serve me. I really . . .

. . . For those concerned, I am now forty feet up in the branches of a fantrum tree trying to catch my breath. (Stream,) the tall sycophant with the black stripe running down the back of his head, grabbed my book and read aloud to everyone the part about

IT IS OBVIOUS THAT STREAM + CLOVER DO NOT GET ALONG.

me wanting to be a nit so Lilly could serve me.

I'm not sure if Lilly heard. I mean, it could just be a coincidence that she began sobbing and ran off right about that same time. I had to bite Stream on the leg to get my book back. Unfortunately, Professor Winsnicker had just stepped outside to, as he put it, whistle a song so as to make our environment cheery.

When he saw me biting into Stream, he ceased whistling and ran over to break us up. I have never seen him so mad. He actually screamed at me. He was ranting about biting and how sycophants must never bite one another. I think I actually saw steam coming from his ears.

I grabbed my book and

I WONDER IF. . . I'D BEST NOT WRITE IT DOWN.

climbed as high as I could. Now I'm even more confused and more sweaty.

I think as soon as everyone clears out I'll climb down and run until I find some water to swim in. I'm not sure I'm cut out for this higher education.

Clover from above

CHAPTER EIGHT

SYCOPHANT RUN AND YOUR COMMITMENT

I believe if you know one thing by now it is that I do not like to brag. It makes me uneasy to point out all the many accomplishments I have achieved. However, to eliminate any confusion, I have included a list of things I have been given credit for at the end of this book. Study them carefully. It might be wise to mark a few of the dates and achievements down on your calendar.

Now, where were we? Oh yes, one of my greatest accomplishments: visiting and living here on Sycophant Run. The very fact that I am now

91

It might be wise to mark a few of the dates and achievements down on your calendar, especially my birthday.

instructing you is nothing short of amazing. In the history of Foo there has never been a nit that has had such access to and love from the sycophants as I. I consider it one of your greatest traits, the fact that you as a breed recognized the importance of including me.

Perhaps it was the wonderful relationship I had with Harold. Maybe it was all the books I had studied and facts I had retained. I'll even concede that it could have had something to do with my ship being shipwrecked upon your shores and you showing mercy on me after I begged you to let me live.

COULD THEY ACTUALLY KILL HIM?

Let's not fight over the whys.

Let's just agree to let me say that whatever great things I have achieved—including those I did but have never been acknowledged for—it doesn't matter. What is most important is that the sycophants have taken me in like a brother.

My time on Sycophant Run has been most eye-opening.

It is now abundantly clear just how important this place is. I have only one thing to say:

Guard it with your life.

Fate allowed you to let me stay, but fate also knows how dangerous the invasion of outsiders would be. In the history of Foo there have been many attacks and attempts to storm your shores. Always, the invisibility and sheer numbers of sycophants have easily thwarted and kept at bay any who wished to do you harm. Because I am so brave, I would dare say that there are few borders anywhere in Foo or Reality so fiercely guarded and protected.

As you well know, every sycophant is required to spend five years living as a peg posted on the shore of Sycophant Run. You should know this, because you have done it already. One of the prerequisite requirements for my class, besides your having had your twelve years of learning how to write and add, is that you have already served your time as a peg. Being a posted peg is a great responsibility and an important duty. It is also the crucial development time for you and your claws. I won't go into this, seeing as how you have already experienced it.

CLAWS? I'M CONFUSED.

Suffice it to say, Sycophant Run is an important place.

Most who live and die in Foo know very little about Sycophant Run. They know it is there, across the Veil Sea, shrouded by the mists. Few have even seen its outline or silhouette, but many have heard laughter or other noises coming from your land. I now know many of the reasons why you laugh and the source of some of those noises. I also know why you guard your land so fiercely.

Take comfort in the fact that not even death would loose my lips.

Sycophant Run is your haven, your strength, and Foo's biggest secret. As someone mentioned earlier, I am very brave, but even I dare not pen some of the things I now know about Sycophant Run and its importance to the dreams and hopes of all mankind. I am forced to tell you things verbally—things that you will be instructed never to write down. Your obedience to this law is crucial.

Let's talk.

I know, it's a lot to take in. Think about everything I have said. Do not discuss it with friends, chums, pals, family, and certainly not acquaintances. Sycophant Run and the fate of all mankind and their dreams depend on it.

Since you shouldn't write about any of this, use this time to write about something you have learned previously from me.

EXTRA SPECIAL WRITING TIME.

Dear Book,

I don't know what to do. I feel like everything in my life has been put into a can, shaken up, and then dumped out. Professor Winsnicker said some unbelievable things this lesson. I have always known how important Sycophant Run is, but I didn't realize that we as sycophants are hiding and maintaining so many important secrets. I suppose I could better deal with all this if it weren't for the turmoil in Foo at the moment. According to the Scroll, dreams are getting darker, and more and more of those who live in Foo are talking about finding a way out.

Escaping Foo!

Who in their right mind would want such

a thing? There is even talk of a man who has already slipped away!

All of this would not be so upsetting if I hadn't learned what I just did about Sycophant Run. It seems as if we sycophants bear a lot of the load.

On top of all of this, Lilly isn't even materializing around me anymore. I heard one of her friends say that she was thinking of not finishing school so she can spend more time helping her mother. Noble, sure, but I don't know what I would do without the possibility of seeing her.

Two more sycophants from our class have up and disappeared. I feel like Professor Winsnicker isn't very concerned about them being gone. He claims they have run off to find their first burns. I think he's just too lazy to do anything about it.

It was a bit painful to talk about our time as pegs on the shore. Those were not the best years of my life. I suppose I would feel better about things <u>if I had developed claws.</u> Most sycophants grow claws while they are posted as pegs guarding the borders of Sycophant Run. Usually the claws are about six inches long, but I had friends who had claws as long as ten inches.

I WONDERED WHY CLOVER HAD NEVER MENTIONED CLAWS.

Mine, unfortunately, never developed or even showed up. I still don't like to think about it. During Professor Winsnicker's class, Stream spoke up and pointed out to everyone how I had never grown claws during my duty. I argued that all sycophants lose their claws after serving anyway, but Stream just called me defective. I wish he'd disappear for good.

I can't believe how many things I am holding in my head.

I sent a personal lob to my mother. There are some things about Sycophant Run that trouble me. I have always thought our land was a magical place filled with possibility and complete security. Now, I am confused.

My head hurts.

Baffled,

Clover-Dreadfully-Ernest

CHAPTER NINE

APPROPRIATE PLACES TO SIT

What we are going to talk about now might seem a little old-fashioned or out-of-date, but I believe it is every bit as important today as it was in years past. It may be considered quite "hip" to sit where you please on your burn, but that doesn't make it right. A well-mannered sycophant knows what is appropriate and what is not.

During the earliest days of Foo, all sycophants stayed ten paces behind their burns at all times.

As the wars in Foo escalated, the need for sycophants to provide greater comfort to their burns

THE EARLY WARS THAT BROUGHT AN END TO METAL.

increased. It just wasn't enough for them simply to hang back ten feet. Sycophants suddenly needed to pet and soothe their burns.

As dreams began to get more and more selfish, sycophants and their therapist role grew. As each day plays out, it seems as if the quality of nits freshly snatched into Foo is growing less and less impressive. Some nits need years of counseling and consoling before they can even begin to see incoming dreams or understand their gifts.

In days gone by we could count on the Council

of Wonder and Council of Whisps to regulate and
control the tone of Foo. Now, however, there are
some who talk openly of Foo being something that
it wasn't meant to be. There is even talk of taking our
gifts and returning to Reality.

Rubbish.

How hard-headed people can be at times!

The point of this tirade is to express that times
have changed. What was bright and simple is growing dark and complicated. Good is sometimes little
more than a memory, and evil is invited to places and
situations from which it was previously banned.

MORFIT

And even though some traits and characteristics
of the sycophant have evolved, there are still some
things that should not be tampered with.
Sycophants are to respect their burns. They are to
walk with them and whisper things that will make
their nits believe in themselves and adapt to Foo.
They are to strengthen the will and desire of nits
so that they might miraculously and marvelously
enhance the dreams of those in Reality.

* A NUMBER OF ITS MEMBERS HAVE BEEN
BURIED IN THE SWOLLEN FOREST.

Be true to your instincts. You are the glue that holds the dreams of all mankind together.

Nowadays it is very much in fashion to sit on the shoulders of the one you burn for—in fashion and, I must add, appropriate. Upper back is also considered dignified and modest. I have seen incidents in which clinging to the ankle was necessary and admissible, but that is about it.

Times change, and I have always been one to connect with the youth and their movements. Hence, I have come to believe that resting on shoulders, upper backs, or ankles is completely acceptable.

But, there are places that even I in my open-mindedness simply cannot tolerate. Only the most disobedient sycophant rests on the head of his or her burn. Clinging to arms is also forbidden. Nits need their arms and hands to work with dreams—if there is a delinquent sycophant hanging onto their wrists, how can they properly manipulate?

It is a lowly sycophant who parks his or her behind on the top of a burn's feet. This causes undue

Circle the appropriate places to sit on your burn.

difficulty for your nit as he or she tries to walk. Clinging to the side or front of your burn is still considered an invasion of personal space.

I know there are sycophants who think nothing of hanging on and sitting all over their burns, but despite what they say or how they rationalize it, such behavior is out of line and inappropriate and the sign of a naughty, naughty sycophant. Here's a little rhyme I once heard a group of young sycophants using while playing rotscotch:

> Shoulders, ankles, upper back.
> If you're on those then you're on track.

See, even young sycophants can contribute. Of course, they were all fresh from one of my lessons.

LET'S BREAK AND GIVE THE INFORMATION A CHANCE TO SEEP IN.

Mr. Diary,

I am so concerned. I don't feel like the same sycophant who started this course all that while ago. I sweat a lot now. My nose itches, my eyes are watery, and I think my hair is growing at a faster rate than usual. Two days ago I think I felt lonely.

I've never really felt lonely before.

CLOVER IS DEFINITELY CHANGING!

Almost every other night I wake up running toward the far shore of Sycophant Run. I received a personal lob back from my mother last night. She told me to wait out the changes and to not worry about Sycophant Run or all the secrets we hide.

She also said that if I was wise and kept myself in line, someday I would be a great sycophant.

The most depressing part of my life is that Lilly has gone. She didn't return to help her mother, she felt the pull of a burn and ran off two days ago. She's probably halfway across the Veil Sea by now.

No good-bye, no see you later, nothing.

Lilly ran off with three other sycophants. I'm beginning to feel like this school is just a place to corral us until fate compels us to leave. I told Professor Winsnicker that and he patted me on the head harder than he ever has before.

I can't believe, with all the things Professor Winsnicker is telling us, and with all that is going on around us in Foo and in the dreams of mankind, that we are still getting lessons on where to sit. Who cares

where we sit? I'm sure I'll always walk ten
paces behind my burn. Who wants to ride on
someone's shoulders?

It is a cold time of the year. The fantrum
trees are exchanging leaves and the fish
around the shore of Sycophant Run are
jumping from the water in large clusters and
making it look as if the entire sea is
fizzing.

A strong Lore Coil drifted across our
land whispering of a recent attempt to kill
the Want. The best I could decipher the news
was that the Want weathered the attack and
is alive and more angry than ever. The
dreams coming into Foo seem to be shakier
and less spectacular than those of just a
few years ago.

I'm lonely, and my legs want to run.

ONLY THE STRONGEST
LORE COILS MAKE IT CLEARLY
THROUGH THE MISTS OF THE VEIL SEA.

I wish I was a stant so I could tip my head back and howl.

Alas, I'm just,

Clover the sycophant

CHAPTER TEN

AFTER THE INITIAL BURN: REMAINING COMMITTED

This is a selfish chapter. By selfish I mean that I will be telling you things here that are for your benefit and yours alone—things that will make your life considerably easier. Please try not to abuse the knowledge.

Have you ever enjoyed an exceptionally delicious piece of pie? I have. There is a small pub on the outskirts of Cork that makes the most delicious fableberry pie. Of course, if you don't chew the blasted pie just right, you'll end up with large chunks of giggling berries lodged in your throat.

111

I really love that pie.

However, I'm sure if I were served fableberry pie every day of my life, I would grow a bit tired of it. Yes, I would be cordial and say that I was enjoying it, but the truth is, I would likely be hankering for a serving of something else.

You might find it a stretch, but your burn is not so different from that pie. There will be moments when you are so happy to be around the one you burn for, you can hardly believe your luck. There might even be days and weeks and months when you feel nothing but bliss. But there will also be times when, as with that pie, you wish you could have some variety.

Don't worry. The feelings you are experiencing are as normal as any sycophant feelings can be. Might I suggest that you try to get your burn to do something that will freshen things up?

There was a time years ago when Harold spent three weeks trying to convince me to part my hair on the opposite side, just to add a little flare to our friendship. To appease him I changed my part, and I must admit that for the next little while it made things feel much more new and fresh.

Little things can make a big difference. Here are a few ideas:

Suggest that your burn wear glasses.

Have your burn take up a hobby that will entertain you.

If your burn is a male, talk about how cool goatees look.

If your burn is a female, talk about how attractive big hair is.

You watch: They will take your suggestions to heart, and soon their small changes will make your relationship exciting again. I know of a nit who changed the hand he wrote with just to appease his sycophant. Once, when I knew Harold was having a particularly hard day, I came home wearing my felt hat at a jaunty angle, and it changed his mood completely.

The sycophant-burn relationship can last many

THE MANY FACES OF PROFESSOR WINSNICKER

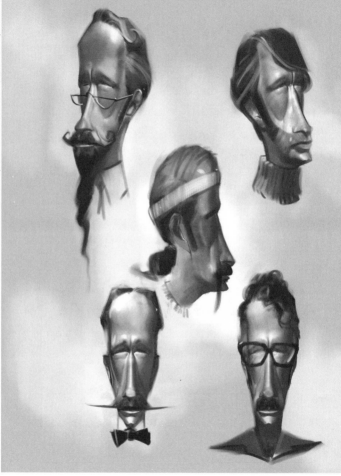

I believe that keeping appearances fresh and exciting will improve any sycophant-burn relationship.

years. There is no law suggesting that the first years should be the best. With a little work and creativity, you can help make the entire time you spend with your burn more fulfilling and fun.

Of course, there will be times when it is absolutely necessary for you to bite your burn and spend some time on yourself. That's okay. Your bite is there for you to use, and it is always a happy reunion when you wake your burn back up.

You owe it to yourself and to your burn to keep things interesting and fun. It takes some nits a lifetime to adjust to Foo, and it might just take that long for them to fully adjust to you.

SELFISH TIME IS OVER.
NOW WRITE A FEW THINGS.

Hey, Book,

Foo is changing. We are isolated here on Sycophant Run, but I can feel that things are shifting. There is a name floating across the air and in weak Lore Coils: Sabine. I asked Professor Winsnicker who Sabine was, and he told me that some things were best never talked about. I asked him how I could possibly learn things if I never talked about them, and he told me to take out a piece of paper and draw a picture of a tree.

SUCH A MESSY WAY TO GET NEWS!

I think his teaching style is wearing thin.

I have woken up the last four nights running toward the far shore of Sycophant Run. I have come to the conclusion that fate

is preparing me to meet and find my burn. I
think I'm okay with this. I still see images
of a boy in my head and I still wish I could
simply become an egg and live with the
Eggmen beneath the Devil's Spiral.

ONGOING?

How about this for a candy? A pit of
caramel . . .

Ahhhhh. It's no good, I can't even focus
on candy because I can feel the pull again. I
think I should forget my last few classes
and take the trip across the Veil Sea now. I
would do it in a second, but it would break
my mother's heart.

It is awful to sit in class and listen to
how we should be committed to our burns
when I can't even go yet. I couldn't care less
what side my burn parts his hair on, I just
want to help Foo. I think something
Professor Winsnicker hasn't really touched
upon is how, although we burn for our burns,

BRILLIANT
+
TRUE

[our true desire is all based on the fact that we burn for Foo.] We sycophants know how important dreams are and how crucial Foo is to dreams.

I told Professor Winsnicker my thoughts, and he told me that it is inappropriate for a student to teach the teacher.

The only good thing about this last set of lessons was the surprise guest: one of Foo's greatest lithens visited our class. His name is Zale, and he came to Sycophant Run to talk with our leaders. I have heard stories for years about Zale and his brother (Geth,) and to finally see him was the best part of anything I've learned. He told us how Foo needed us now more than ever. I then told him about what I had been feeling concerning sycophants ultimately burning for Foo.

IS
ZALE
OLDER?

He called me most remarkable and a sycophant to watch.

I don't know what to make of everything. I can barely sit still for even a moment. I definitely feel like I have changed from who I was when I first began school. I look at my hands and my feet and have a hard time recognizing myself. It's as if a giant wave of something is racing toward me and I have no way of holding it back. I worry about myself a little, but mostly I hope there is something I can do for Foo.

Head full of gray,

Clov

it's blue
today
blue again!

CHAPTER ELEVEN

FALLING IN LOVE AND FAMILY LIFE

Let me preface this chapter by inviting you to please calm down. Yes, we will be talking about love and falling in such, but I believe we can discuss it in a civilized and nontitillating manner. We are all mature and sophisticated. Love shouldn't change our vocabulary or our sense of appropriateness.

Here's the good news. Fate would not deny any of you the chance to spot a beautiful or handsome sycophant from across the room, lock eyes with that sycophant, and then exchange pedigree info and file with the Sycophant Office of Love and Blushing.

All unions and relationships are recorded and watched over by the Sycophant Office of Love and Blushing, or SOLB.

Your breed likes to know who's making eyes at whom.

I credit your leaders with this notion. It is an organized system that the sycophants use to facilitate love. You get all the romance with a built-in infrastructure. All unions and relationships are recorded and watched over by the Sycophant Office of Love and Blushing, or SOLB.

As you have gained knowledge over this long course, you have probably come to realize just how important sycophants are. This is why SOLB has such a keen interest in what you all are up to in the love department.

Despite all you will do in your lifetime, if you desire it, you will find love. I am frequently asked, "But how can I fall in love when I am attached to a burn?"

Most sycophants will stay with and assist a burn until that burn passes on. Then, if you wish, you can return to Sycophant Run and register with SOLB, wait two weeks for a certified form to arrive by lob,

TAKES A FEW HOURS TO
ARRIVE ONCE SENT.

fill out said form, tie the mating ring to the left hem of your robe to signify your availability, comb yourself thoroughly with a Professor Winsnicker's Patented Grooming Comb, draw a picture of the type of sycophant you would like to marry, and from there simply let the spontaneous and wondrous course of love begin.

Now, it's true that some sycophants never marry. That's their prerogative. Some marry after multiple burns. Some are just picky and still looking. Some have lost permission to pursue from SOLB. But the majority of sycophants will serve burns and then return to Sycophant Run to find love. I have always liked the poetic expression I read on a sycophant washroom stall years ago:

> Wendell and Fern sitting in a fantrum tree
> B-L-U-S-H-I-N-G
> First comes registering, then comes
> approval,
> Then comes Wendell drawing wedding
> doodles.

Love can be so innocent and sweet.

When I met my wonderful wife, I didn't have the option of having an entire organization looking over my shoulder to make sure I was falling in love properly. You're quite lucky.

The Sycophant Office of Love and Blushing has asked me to include this next bit.

Hooray for the Sycophant Office of Love and Blushing!

Seems a bit forced, if you ask me, but seeing how I am not one to challenge tradition, I see no problem with you reading that cheer over and over and repeating it to yourself when you are alone or with a big group of friends.

The problem I *have* always had with that cheer is that it doesn't include a single reference to me and what I have taught you. Feel free to massage the message if you want. Here's a suggestion just off the top of my head.

Hooray for all the many amazing things Professor Winsnicker has taught us!

Again, just a suggestion, but I think it still conveys what the SOLB was trying to say.

What's most important, however, is to remember that fate wants you to live a happy and fulfilling life. Burning for a nit is not a punishment; it is in your blood. Since the creation of time, it has been your role to selflessly balance and secure this amazing realm. Many don't give you the credit you deserve, but from early on I have noticed and commented on how grateful I am for all that the sycophants do. Someday, when the history of Foo is complete, and light is but a memory in the minds of all who have lived and died, the word *sycophant* will be as honored as any other. And will be listed above mine.

How True!

If they list them alphabetically.

Thank you for your goodness. Know that you will find love and potentially live forever, and that you and your offspring will shape the future of Foo as you have helped shape the beginning.

I am touched by who you are and what I have written.

GIVE ME A MOMENT TO COMPOSE MYSELF.

For my eyes only,
    I woke last night by
falling from my (bind) up
in the fantrum tree and
hitting the ground hard.
    I thought it was my
restless soul that had thrown
me from bed, but according to Professor
Winsnicker, the siids were on the move,
changing the balance of Foo again. This
morning the sky was filled with thick black
streaks. I hope the siids find a more harmonic
balance than we have been experiencing.
    Professor Winsnicker has been teaching us
about love and passing around a petition to
create a new holiday called Winsnicker Day.
We each signed the petition while he looked

NOT A VERY COMFORTABLE WAY TO SLEEP.

over our shoulders. I suppose you can't have too many holidays.

It doesn't matter anyway; I'm going to be leaving soon. I know, it came as a surprise to me as well. Zale came back after spending time with the elders of Sycophant Run to find me. I was confused at first, then more confused, and then honored. But I turned from honored to scared when he informed me that he had come to take me away because there was someone he needed me to burn for. Apparently there is a young nit new to Foo who has, for reasons Zale couldn't explain, failed to attract a single sycophant. Zale said the nit's name was <u>Antsel</u> and that he was a great person.   AMAZING!

Antsel.

It's not Lilly, but then again, what is? I told Zale that I couldn't leave until I

finished school, and he said I had great
integrity.

He had no idea how wrong he was. So I
told him. I told him that I think about candy
all the time, that I daydream on top of my
daydreams, that I find leaves to be better
friends than other sycophants, that I think
Professor Winsnicker just might not be the
greatest teacher of all time, that I took
that pamphlet from Winsnicker's desk and
still haven't given it back and really have no
intention of ever giving it back, that I find
old people funny and young people frightening,
that I think of myself all the time and
wonder what I would look like with a thick
blond mustache . . .

. . . that I am in love with Lilly and I
haven't said a word about it to
the Sycophant Office of Love
and Blushing, that when other
people talk I usually tune
out, that I never could grow
claws, that I want to be an
egg, and that I used to not
want a burn or anything to do
with one.

I said a few other things, but I
don't want to completely humiliate myself in
writing. When I was done spilling my guts,
Zale just laughed and asked me if I loved
Foo.

I told him I did, with all my heart. AS DO I.

He replied, Perfect, and promised that he
would be back for me when my studies had
ended. He then gave me a really fascinating
twig that he had found the day before.

I have sent a personal lob to my mother and father telling them what is happening. I hope they understand.

I wish I was an herbalist living in a small cottage with Lilly.

Chapter Twelve

Keeping Secrets and Avoiding Epiphanies

We are nearing the end. I believe I can hear the sound of sycophant weeping. Bless you and your soft heart. Don't worry, though, you will always have your textbook to look back at. You will also see me walking your streets and may feel free to approach me and ask me any question you wish.

What a bright future you have before you.

We have talked and laughed and learned a lot of wonderful things. Think about how much more you now know. It has been my pleasure to spend this time with you.

We have touched upon important topics in this course. You've learned the fundamentals of grooming yourself and the origin of your most precious possession—your robe. We talked about you finding the perfect burn, but also about how fate will set you up in ways you might not understand. I pulled no punches as I pointed at you and insisted you stay invisible and out of the way when you should. I let you in on the power of your bite and how miraculous your choppers are. I whispered and warned you about staying away from metal and how the very future of Foo depends on it. !!

We talked and sighed about changing your name and how exciting that can be. You listened intently as we covered the importance of making your burn feel at ease, and I entrusted you with secret information concerning your home—Sycophant Run. You now know where to sit and how to keep your relationship with your burn fresh and fun. We talked seriously about love and the SOLB. And throughout it all I have poured out my heart and rolled up my sleeves both figuratively and literally during that particularly hot spell we went through.

We are kindred spirits, you and I. You have let me into your world, and I have graciously accepted. There are many more truths I could teach you, but for now take comfort in the assurance that you know the most important things for this stage of your life. There is just one more idea I would like to cover before you step out into the world: the importance of keeping secrets. — HE NEVER MENTIONS KEYS

Many of the problems and hiccups of Foo have come about by people's speaking up when they should have kept quiet. The Swollen Forest is filled with buried secrets that should never have gotten out in the first place. You, my friends, hold more secrets than any others in Foo. Not only will you know information about your burns, but you know of Sycophant Run, and you know by instinct of the greatest secret of Foo—how a sycophant dies.

You must never speak of these things.

Never.

There will be many who spend their time doing nothing but trying to draw secrets from you. Those who will try the hardest are the tricky epiphanies. They will sneak into your life and present themselves as a new understanding or a wonderful revelation— at which point they hope you will feel comfortable enough to spill your guts.

Don't do it.

If the situation seems too comfortable, it probably is. Epiphanies are sneaky, but it takes only one hard pinch to cause them to show their true colors. Before they have you in a trance, reach out and pinch them as hard as you can. This will most likely elicit a short spout of vulgar language, followed by kicking and screaming, but soon they will give up and drift off.

Epiphanies want nothing but your discomfort.

They would take your dearest secret and trade it

*Don't be fooled. Drifting epiphanies are sneaky
and will try to draw secrets from you.*

to the tharms of the Swollen Forest for a handful of berries.

Avoid them if possible. Don't hang out near still water or under rainbows. These are epiphany breeding grounds and dangerous places for sycophants to be. Your secrets belong to you and your breed. Keep them safe.

Stay away from the borders of Foo. The epiphanies are curious and always looking for ways to breach the borders.

Most epiphanies won't approach you if you are in the vicinity of your burn. They like to get you alone. Also, they are painfully aware that most burns can pinch much harder than sycophants. This is an added incentive for you to stay close to your burn and always be aware of your surroundings.

If you will exercise a little judicious caution, epiphanies will be nothing but a nuisance to you. So far they have been unable to trick a single sycophant into divulging your deepest secrets. Fate is waiting it out with us. But this is no reason to relax into carelessness—the tiniest epiphany can become a great deterrent of Foo.

They are your secrets, so keep them safe.

I have nothing more to say at the moment.

UNUSUAL FOR
WINSNICKER

Your final thoughts.

To whom it may concern,

Zale is here. He showed up two days after my last class. I gave him a whole new list of reasons why I wouldn't be a good sycophant for Antsel, but he promised me I would be exceptional. I used to think he was smart.

Professor Winsnicker is so proud that one of his pupils will be going with Zale. He said he hadn't been so moved since they announced that Winsnicker Day will be a Foo-wide holiday.✱

I would be more nervous if it weren't for Zale. Having a lithen of his size to help me along makes me feel like I can do almost anything.

Sycophant Run is in a whirl. Sabine and

✱ SYCOPHANTS CELEBRATE IT MUCH MORE ZEALOUSLY THAN NITS DO.

boatloads of rants tried to storm our
shores last night. We weren't expecting it,
and Sabine actually reached our sand before
the signal was sounded and every sycophant
around attacked. Sabine put up a good fight,
but, as Professor Winsnicker once said, our
invisibility makes us unbeatable. The invisibility helps, but it was the <u>claws of all the
posted pegs</u> that really tore into and
frightened the enemy. A sycophant's claws
can't kill a nit or a rant, but they can
wound it to the point where it is helpless
for many weeks. It took only a short while
before Sabine was heading back out to sea
with his army. I hope he never tries to come
back. Zale said he thinks the only thing
that will stop someone like Sabine from
ruining Foo is a powerful sycophant.
   For the moment I'm pretending that's me.
I will meet Antsel in a couple of days,

once we make it across the Veil Sea. I am
nervous but excited. Zale promised me that
if I don't like him we can call the deal off.

CLOVER
HAD A
WAY OUT.

    I saw Lilly today. She had come back while
her burn rested under the spell of her bite.
I heard her burn was an old woman who was
near death. I guess fate sets us up where
we belong. Maybe Lilly will get a younger
burn next time around.   **WINTER**

    I will miss my family, but I know I'll be
able to return to Sycophant Run many times.
I only hope I can do something with myself
to make them proud.

    I wonder what lies ahead of me. I guess
it's in the hands of fate.
    Nervously,

CLOVER

A WORD OF WARNING

PROFESSOR WINSNICKER KEEPING IT REAL

Surprise! It is I. Think of this afterword as being like a dear friend hidden behind your door quietly waiting to tell you more. You might pretend that I am whispering it to you. I'm sure that will add to the overall feeling of excitement.

When I was snatched into Foo, my whole life changed. It was the beautiful sycophants who helped make me what I am today. Like flour in a cake, you are very rarely given the credit for making Foo such a delicious place. That's a shame. At times I catch myself wishing I could send out millions of locusts with the message of how Foo and Reality owe you a debt of gratitude they can most likely never repay.

Many amazing things have happened and will yet happen in Foo, and you, my dearest friends, will most certainly be a part of those things. And when the day comes that I pass away, I hope that my Harold finds some comfort in the fact that I have been nothing but grateful. I know that if he finds another burn it will be quite hard for the burn to live up to what I have been, but I'm sure Harold will make him feel like he has a value all his own.

Sometimes I worry about Foo.

AMEN! It is the miracle of the sycophants that fills my heart with hope.

Thank you.

Until all dreams are strong and clear,

Professor Philip Winsnicker

HERE IS THE SHORT LIST OF MY ACCOMPLISHMENTS THAT YOU ASKED FOR

SHORT LIST OF ACCOMPLISHMENTS

Born breach. Talked at three months. Walked at nine months. Can blow a bubble inside of a bubble. Champion whistler. Able to guess people's ages within five years plus or minus. Once clapped for two straight days. Excellent negotiator. Was once called on to help the city of Cusp and the city of Cork get along. Has ridden a siid. Has traveled all of Foo. One of the few who has ever stepped onto Sycophant Run. Can hold his breath under water for three minutes. Discovered a new color: plud. Has won multiple medals: one for tight lips, one for an honest face, one for a twenty-four-hour reflective gaze, one for making skipping competitive. Found two four-leaf clovers. Almost swam across the Lime Sea but was stopped due to a leg cramp brought on by swimming too soon after a meal. Has run with the palehi. Counseled with the whisps. Dined with the rants. Has shown equal interest in both nits and cogs. Author of more than 130 books: *Look at Me; Wow, Did I Do That?; How Is It Possible—Let Me Explain; Sycophants: Their Traditions and Customs; Everybody with Me Now?; Listen; Big Heart, Skilled Hands; They Like Me, and Why Shouldn't They?; The Dark State of Dreams: Finding a Solution to Selfishness; Poetic Poems; My Time in Reality; What I Know That You Should Know Too;* and *Smiling, the Forgotten Negotiator,* just to name a few. Once stared directly at the sun. Has met the Want between four and six times. Helped remodel the grand hall of Morfit. Pronounces words perfectly.

Cares for trees and because he does will end this list right here. For more accomplishments check the bulletin board by the main hall. List will be updated as time permits.

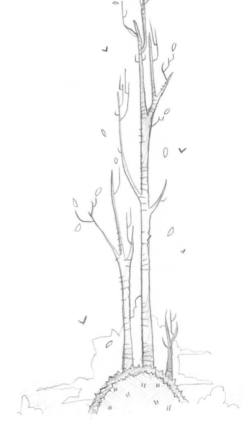

I am so scared. I think this is it. I have been locked in this room for two days wondering if Antsel will ever return. He put me here for my own safety, but I feel like a prisoner. I don't know what to do. For the first time in many years I miss Sycophant Run horribly. It feels like if I were there everything would be okay.

I'm hoping these aren't the last words I ever write as Antsel's burn. He has to be okay. Foo is a mess, but Antsel must be okay. Sabine has grown from a young, power-hungry kid to a vicious dark lord who finds satisfaction and pleasure in the worst of things. The movement to find the gateway Hector Thumps once slipped through has caught the fancy of every rant in Foo. Sabine's armies are large and stupid.

A weak Lore Coil passed over me an hour ago, and if the words are true, Zale is

dead, tricked into death by Sabine. I can
hardly believe it! One of Foo's greatest
defenders has been caught and destroyed. The
coil also spoke of Zale's brother Geth being
cursed to the point of death. I am certain
Antsel is in full pursuit, trying to find out
if the coil is true.

Before Antsel left, he warned me that the
time had come for me to be more than I now
am. He said there was a task for me that
could change the course of all dreams. I don't
care about any task, I only want Antsel to
be okay. He has been my burn for many
years now, and I don't know what I would do
without him.

He also commanded me before he left to
empty my void and be prepared to run on a
moment's notice. I took almost everything out
but the candy. It was while emptying my void
that I came upon my old schoolbook. Those

TRAPPED
IN A
SEED

were such different days. Professor Winsnicker passed away years ago, and I haven't seen Lilly since the day after Sabine's attack on Sycophant Run. I heard she burns for a powerful woman by the name of Winter now.

I can hear screaming outside the door. It sounds as if even the stars are fighting. The moon might have to step in and put an end to this. The walls feel warm, like fire is raging around the home.

Antsel.

There isn't much light, but I can see through a crack near the hinge that someone is right outside the door. I hope it's Antsel, if so, then I will go on living. Of course I will be doing something bigger than what I am doing now.

It is Antsel. He is whispering my name

CHOKED ON AN OLIVE

and telling me to keep quiet. He says we'll
be leaving soon.

I hope I'm ready.

The doorknob is . . .

Dear whoever,

I don't know who I am writing to. Antsel
is gone, and I am alone in Reality. I don't
know too much about why I'm here. I am to
wait for a boy who is soon to be born, and
I'm supposed to take care of him so that he
can go to Foo on some faraway day. Antsel
told me it is the most important mission
any sycophant has ever undertaken.

That doesn't make me feel better.

I tried to see what the gateway was like
as Antsel and I slipped through with what
was left of Geth. But Antsel kept me hidden
beneath his robes. We came out underwater,
and Antsel had to swim like mad to get us
to the top. Even on land he wouldn't take me
out of the robe and let me see where I was.
That's probably wise, but it still drives me
crazy.

I have made a small home out of mud and

LEV!

}— KONIG
   SEA

I FOUND THIS EMPTY MUD HOME
HIDDEN WELL ON THE OKLAHOMA PRAIRIE.

am waiting for the day when the boy will be born. I have lots of candy in my void, and I've been able to find some very agreeable leaves and bark to eat. There are a few beasts around that make me uneasy, so I just stay invisible and out of the way.

I know something is coming. I only hope I can handle it. My hands are shaking now with my thinking and worrying about what is ahead.

Doing this for Antsel,

Clover in Reality

Dear old and comforting book,

It has been a long time since I last opened your covers. The years have gone remarkably fast: faster than my entire childhood, school days, or time in the service of Sycophant Run. The boy I now burn for is named Leven Thumps. He lives in a wide house with two of the meanest people I have ever met. One is a woman and the other is a man, but both are awful.

VERY TRUE!

Leven is twelve and sleeps on the back porch. I have yet to show myself to him, due to the instructions Antsel gave me. It has been so hard not to appear and help him. Okay, if I'm being completely honest, I have to admit that I did show myself once, but only because I thought it would help.

Leven was four, and his guardians had let him cry out on the porch for a full day. As it grew dark, the ugly man guardian, Terry, finally came out and told Leven a story about a young boy who was eaten by a monster because he cried too much. So maybe it was a bad time to appear, but after Terry went in I showed up on Leven's chest to try to comfort him. I had no idea a four-year-old could spring that high or turn that white. I made my way out of there as fast as I could. I didn't think I had done any permanent harm, but since that day Leven has had a handsome white streak in the right side of his dark hair.

CLOVER'S FAULT!

I am waiting for the day when I can properly show myself and tell him I'm sorry. I am happy to be his burn. He is a kind and quiet boy who keeps most of his thoughts to himself. Sometimes I wonder why he is as important as Antsel said. But sometimes,

when he stands tall, I can see something
bigger than what he now is.

The days are warm and lazy. I hope that
the next few years bring something exciting.

I can't wait to see what fate has in
mind.

Clover from Foo

INDEX

G

H

Y

Yale University, alma mater of Professor
    Winsnicker, 19